Dear Parent:

Congratulations! Your child is taking the first steps on an exciting journey. The destination? Independent reading!

STEP INTO READING® will help your child get there. The program offers five steps to reading success. Each step includes fun stories and colorful art. There are also Step into Reading Sticker Books, Step into Reading Math Readers, Step into Reading Write-In Readers, Step into Reading Phonics Readers, and Step into Reading Phonics First Steps! Boxed Sets—a complete literacy program with something for every child.

Learning to Read, Step by Step!

Ready to Read Preschool–Kindergarten
• big type and easy words • rhyme and rhythm • picture clues
For children who know the alphabet and are eager to begin reading.

Reading with Help Preschool–Grade 1
• basic vocabulary • short sentences • simple stories
For children who recognize familiar words and sound out new words with help.

Reading on Your Own Grades 1–3
• engaging characters • easy-to-follow plots • popular topics
For children who are ready to read on their own.

Reading Paragraphs Grades 2–3
• challenging vocabulary • short paragraphs • exciting stories
For newly independent readers who read simple sentences with confidence.

Ready for Chapters Grades 2–4
• chapters • longer paragraphs • full-color art
For children who want to take the plunge into chapter books but still like colorful pictures.

STEP INTO READING® is designed to give every child a successful reading experience. The grade levels are only guides. Children can progress through the steps at their own speed, developing confidence in their reading, no matter what their grade.

Remember, a lifetime love of reading starts with a single step!

For Gee Gee

Published in the United States by Random House Children's Books, a division of Random House, Inc., New York, and simultaneously in Canada by Random House of Canada Limited, Toronto.

www.stepintoreading.com

Educators and librarians, for a variety of teaching tools, visit us at
www.randomhouse.com/teachers

Library of Congress Cataloging-in-Publication Data
Coxe, Molly.
Big egg / by Molly Coxe. p. cm. — (Step into reading. A step 1 book)
SUMMARY: A mother hen wakes up one morning to find a gigantic egg among the others in her nest and goes in search of the egg's origin.
ISBN 0-679-88126-3 (trade) — ISBN 0-679-98126-8 (lib. bdg.)
[1. Chickens—Fiction. 2. Ostriches—Fiction. 3. Animals—Infancy—Fiction.
4. Domestic animals—Fiction.] I. Title. II. Series: Step into reading. Step 1 book.
PZ7.C839424 Bi 2003 [E]—dc21 2002015105

Printed in the United States of America 30 29 28 27 26 25

STEP INTO READING®

Big Egg

by Molly Coxe

Random House New York

Hen has some eggs.

One is big.

The rest are small.

“This is not my egg!”
says Hen.

“Is it a cat egg?”

"No," says Cat.

“Is it a dog egg?”

"No," says Dog.

“Is it a pig egg?”

“No,” says Pig.

“Is it a cow egg?”

“No,” says Cow.

“Is it a goat egg?”

“No,” says Goat.

"Is it a fox egg?"

"YES!" says Fox.

The small eggs crack.

“Peep! Peep!”

say the small chicks.

The big egg cracks.

"SQUAWK!"

says the big chick.

“Run!” says Hen.

Hen has some chicks.

One is big.

The rest are small.

Hen loves them all.